D1108432

To my parents, Keith and Rose, who
gave me their full attention.

www.mascotbooks.com

Got Any GAMES on your PHONE?

©2020 Joshua White. All Rights Reserved. No part of this publication may be reproduced, stored in a retrieval system or transmitted in any form by any means electronic, mechanical, or photocopying, recording or otherwise without the permission of the author.

For more information, please contact:
Mascot Books
620 Herndon Parkway #320
Herndon, VA 20170
info@mascotbooks.com

Library of Congress Control Number: 2019915970

CPSIA Code: PRT1219A
ISBN-13: 978-1-64543-147-3

Printed in the United States

Got Any GAMES on your PHONE?

Written by **Joshua White**

Illustrated by Agus Prajogo

Legend never wanted to play **outside**.
He's been to the park but never on the **slides**.

Legend didn't like riding skateboards or flying **kites**.
He never played tag or visited a **campsite**.

He was scared of bugs and hated long **hikes**.
What he loved, though, was playing on his
parents' phone all **night**.

He wasn't impressed by bald eagles
or petting his neighbor's **beagle**.
On his mom's phone he felt
the most **peaceful**.

Legend didn't care for sunshine or playing with his **friends**.
He liked being with his phone on the couch in the **den**.

Legend never drank hot chocolate or tried **calamari**.
He even missed an opportunity to go on a **safari**.

Legend just wanted to play on his phone all day. The app store was like a gold **mine**. The phone was becoming Legend's best friend of all **time**.

Then one day, the phone went **black**!
Legend had an anxiety **attack**.

"Mom, help! The battery's **dead**!"
Legend felt a pounding in his **head**.
He fell to the ground because he couldn't feel his **legs**!

"Legend! Legend! Are you **okay**?
We need to get you to the doctor right **away**!"

"Doctor, is Legend going to be **alright**?"
The doctor said, "It's looking worse than a snake **bite**!

He shouldn't be on the phone any **more**.
He needs to explore the great **outdoors**!

The zoo, the park, the basketball **court**.
Legend needs to play every **sport**!

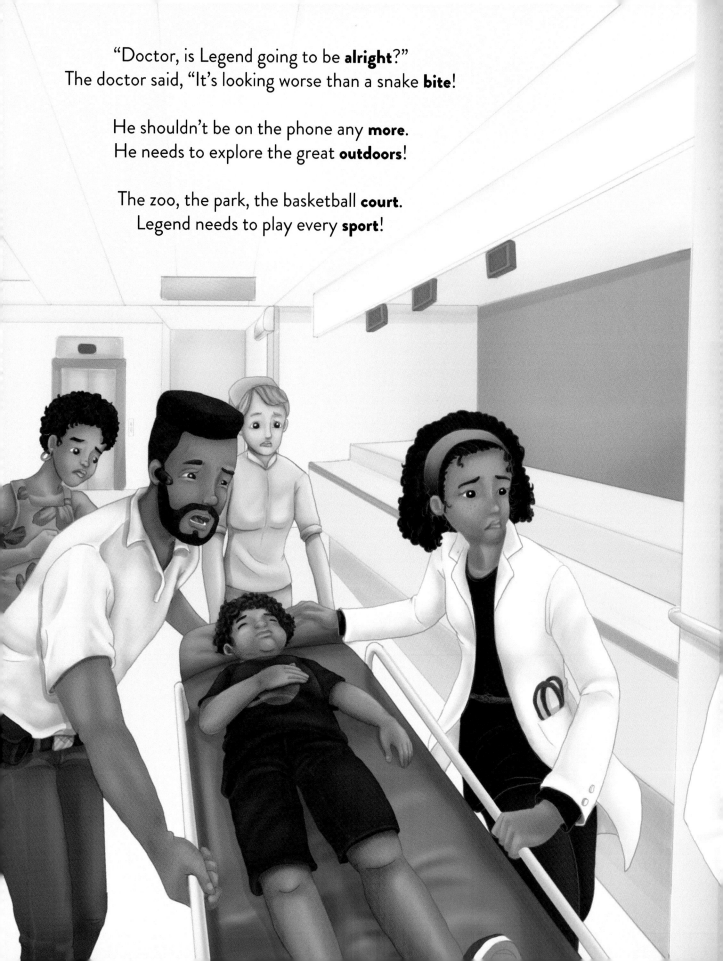

He needs ice cream and a ton of **sugar**.
When's the last time he ate a **booger**?

Take him everywhere! Go tour a **spaceship**.
Jump on a trampoline and do a back **flip**.

Just go have fun outside for a **while**
without your phone, and you'll start to **smile**!"

Legend frowned. "Go outside and get sweat in my **hair**? I'd rather wrestle a grizzly **bear**!

Mom, Mom, this isn't **fair**! Let's get a second opinion **elsewhere**!"

The doctor said, "I've seen this more and **more**. This isn't something you should **ignore**.

When will you see the phone is
really a dead **end**?
Just do as I say and you won't
end up here **again**."

Legend felt sick by the thought of being **outside**
But it was the doctor's orders, so he had to **comply**.

*Outdoors, Legend thought, is so hot and **sticky**.
Maybe I can get a fake mustache and change my name to **Ricky**!*

On the ride home, Legend said, "I don't want to play **outside**,
I just want to play games on your phone. That's not a **crime**!"

His mom said, "In my day, we didn't have phones or **computers**.
We just jumped rope and rode **scooters**!

You know, it wasn't terrible at **all**.
Why don't you try playing a little **basketball**?"

So Legend decided to play basketball with his **dad**.
He shot some hoops and thought, *You know what, this isn't* **bad**.

The fresh air helped clear his **head**.
"I feel better already!" he **said**.

Next, he rode his bike down a **hill**
and his sister showed him how to **grill**.

He played football in the **dirt**
and got grass stains on his knees and **shirt**.

Soon, Legend fell in love with being **outside**.
He read books and collected shells at low **tide**.

Outside, there were so many **festivities**.
The world had an unlimited amount of fun **activities**!

Now Legend is outside all the **time**
and if you ask him, he'll say he feels **fine**!

Legend put the phone **down**
and now he's the coolest kid in **town**!

About the Author

Joshua White calls Northern California home. You can catch him gazing at the universe through his telescope or at your local car meet. He entered Bethune - Cookman University to learn and departed to serve. He enjoys the great outdoors and doesn't have any games on his phone that you can play.